HUNCHBACK

HUNCHBACK

A Novel

SAOU ICHIKAWA

TRANSLATED BY POLLY BARTON

HOGARTH

LONDON • NEW YORK

Originally published in Japan as ハンチバック by 文藝春秋
by Bungeishunju, Tokyo, in 2023. Copyright © 2023 by Saou Ichikawa.

Translation copyright © 2025 by Polly Barton

All rights reserved.

Published in the United States by Hogarth, an imprint of Random House,
a division of Penguin Random House LLC, 1745 Broadway, New York, NY 10019.

HOGARTH is a trademark of the Random House Group Limited,
and the H colophon is a trademark of Penguin Random House LLC.

This translation published in the United Kingdom by Viking,
an imprint of Penguin General. Penguin General is part of
the Penguin Random House group of companies.

LIBRARY OF CONGRESS CATALOGING-IN-PUBLICATION DATA
NAMES: Ichikawa, Saō, author. | Barton, Polly (Translator), translator
TITLE: Hunchback: a novel / Saou Ichikawa; Polly Barton.
OTHER TITLES: Hanchibakku. English
DESCRIPTION: London; New York, NY: Hogarth, 2025.
IDENTIFIERS: LCCN 2024035614 (print) | LCCN 2024035615 (ebook) |
ISBN 9780593734711 (hardcover; acid-free paper) |
ISBN 9780593734735 (ebook)
SUBJECTS: LCSH: Women with disabilities—Fiction. | Women with disabilities—
Social conditions—Fiction. | People with disabilities—Fiction. | People with
disabilities—Social conditions—Fiction. | LCGFT: Novels.
CLASSIFICATION: LCC PL871.5.C548 H3613 2025 (print) |
LCC PL871.5.C548 (ebook) | DDC [FIC]—dc23
LC record available at https://lccn.loc.gov/2024035614
LC ebook record available at https://lccn.loc.gov/2024035615

Printed in Canada on acid-free paper

randomhousebooks.com
penguinrandomhouse.com

2 4 6 8 9 7 5 3 1

FIRST US EDITION

Book design by Barbara M. Bachman

The authorized representative in the EU for product safety and compliance is
Penguin Random House Ireland, Morrison Chambers, 32 Nassau Street,
Dublin D02 YH68, Ireland, https://eu-contact.penguin.ie.

HUNCHBACK

MY STEAMY THREESOME WITH
SUPER-SEXY STUDENTS IN ONE OF
TOKYO'S MOST SOUGHT-AFTER
SWINGERS' CLUBS (PART I)

The place in question was just ten minutes' walk from Shibuya Station.

Spotting the rose slanting across the sign, I knew I'd made it to the Castle of Desire.

But I guess I should introduce myself first, eh? My name's Mikio, and I'm a freelance writer. The mission I'd been set this time was to report under-cover on one of Tokyo's most legendary swingers' clubs. So, without further ado . . .

I stepped through the door with S, a college student I'd matched with on a dating app. When she'd locked eyes with me at our appointed meeting place, she'd shot me a smile that reminded me of that new, effortlessly slick female presenter on one of the major TV channels—in any case, she was super hot. What's more, the tits jutting out from her black turtleneck sweater were an E-cup . . . !

I should probably say at this point that I'm already a member of the swingers' club in question, so there were no problems getting in. Truth is, I used to be a regular, before becoming a writer . . .

The place is made up of three floors. On the first floor is the reception and a locker room, the second floor is the lounge bar, and the third floor is where the playrooms are. It was 8 P.M., and the lounge bar had a nice buzz to it. I'd put the guy-to-girl ratio at about 7:3.

Stripping off and touching in the lounge bar are prohibited, but kissing is okay—those are the house rules. As S and I were chatting over mojitos at one of the booth seats, another couple came up, also with mojitos in hand, and asked us if they could join us.

The guy introduced himself as a thirty-two-year-old trader, very much the jock type. Discovering that S was at Waseda, he revealed that he'd been there himself. The two of them talked up a storm about that for a while, then seamlessly progressed to a steamy make-out session. This dude was clearly no beginner to these kinds of night-spots! In case you're wondering, Mikio graduated from a slightly less illustrious university . . . (^^;)

Someone suggested that we take things to the playroom, so we made our way upstairs. A member of staff pointed the four of us to a room that just so happened to be empty. Luck was on our side!

The girl the trader had brought with him, twenty-six-year-old Y who hailed from Minato— only the most affluent district of Tokyo—said it was her first time at a sex club. She'd had a five-some in high school, though. Some education that must have been, jeez . . . ! The playroom had red plastic matting underfoot, and glass walls on all sides. At a push of the remote button, the trans-parent glass clouded over. Y blew me while I stood there sensing the figures clustered around outside like a bunch of garden gnomes. Man, that felt good! I guess it makes sense that someone who'd had a fivesome in high school would know how to give decent head. Just as she'd gulped down a load of my pre-cum, we switched places. I've got a thing for doing it with clothes on, so I stood behind her and fondled her tits through her blouse as I licked the inside of her ear.

Meanwhile, S was leaning up against the tinted glass while the trader sucked on her E-cup tits. The black turtleneck hoisted up around her mouth muffled her moans so they sounded super horny. Her enormous white breasts were glistening and bouncy like ripe Japanese pears. You had to hand it to twenty-one-year-old college students! Huge but still pert, they really were a flawless set of tits.

No wonder twenty-six-year-old Y was hanging her head, her cheeks reddened by the humiliation of defeat. Although, if I'm being totally honest, I'm not that into big-breasted women. Y's regular-sized, slightly saggy tits were actually way more up my alley. Yeah, she was really turning me on. I stuck a hand into her panties to find she was already dripping wet. "Can I fuck you?" I groaned into her ear. "Sure ♡!" she replied. I grabbed one of the condom packets that had come pirouetting down from the ceiling at just the right moment, and so began Round One. I took her first in the missionary position and she started moaning like the bit in that Matsuken Samba song where Ken's voice flicks up weirdly high at the end of his words. Out of the corner of my eye, I watched the trader fucking S from behind, her palms pressed up against the smoked glass, making her orgasm over and over. Thinking that this crazy samba of ours needed an audience, I reached out a hand for the remote. Beyond the panes of glass that turned clear in an instant stood a whole cluster of garden gnomes doing their one-handed jig.

I saved the document and closed the WordPress editing screen, then set the iPad mini I'd been holding in both hands down onto the toweling blanket drawn across my stomach. While I'd been concentrating on getting to the end of the article, mucus had built up in my windpipe, and the alarm on my Trilogy ventilator was chirruping furiously. I inserted the suction catheter to drain off the mucus—the air entering through the ventilator tube for the best part of twenty minutes had whipped it up to a foamy texture—reconnected the ventilator to my tracheostomy tube, then picked up my iPhone from beside my bed and opened the chat app that I used for work.

> I've just submitted the first half of the
> Swingers' Club piece. Do let me know
> your thoughts when you have a
> moment.

Once again I suctioned off the mucus rising up, and this time, immediately felt the oxygen moving to my brain. Yeah, that felt—good.

> Thanks very much. Can I ask you to
> deliver the second half by the end of the
> week, along with both the Fukuoka and
> Nagasaki editions of the Top 20 Pickup
> Spots?

> > Yes, that's no problem. I'll have all three
> > of them to you by Saturday.

I picked up the iPad mini and once again logged in to WordPress. Among the list of articles created by the editorial department, which were so far just a bunch of titles inserted into templates, I tapped on the words reading "Fukuoka Edition" in order to assign Buddha as editor. That was my account name—Buddha. For twenty-nine years now, I have been residing in

Nirvana. Ever since the day that my underdeveloped muscles had prevented my heart and lungs from maintaining a normal level of oxygen saturation, and I'd grown faint and passed out by the classroom window in my second year of middle school.

That makes it almost thirty years since I stopped walking outside, the soles of my shoes scraping along the pavement.

The hands of the clock on the wall were glancing twelve. Turning my attention to my bladder, I admitted the urge to pee, and so, as burdensome a prospect as it was, I readied myself to get up and use the bathroom. Even Buddha had to rise and walk around Nirvana from time to time, surely. Deflating the trach cuff with a syringe, I detached the ventilator's connector and turned it off before the alarm could sound.

The S-shaped curvature of my spine, twisted so as to crush my right lung, afforded special significance to left and right. I could only get out of bed from the left-hand side. It was easier to get in from the right-hand side, but my head refused to turn in that direction, and so the TV had to be placed on my left. I could only reach the right portion of both the upper and lower shelves of the fridge. Only the very tips of my left toes touched the floor. As a consequence, my way of walking was sufficiently imbalanced to make the word "limp" seem an understatement, and whenever I lost focus, I'd strike my head on the left-hand side of the door frame.

It had happened just this morning, in fact—not paying enough attention, I'd struck my head. The burst of air intended as a scream had leaked out of my tracheostomy tube before it could reach my vocal cords.

"   "

Returning from the bathroom, I reattached to the ventilator. I brought up my private Twitter account on my iPhone and tweeted:

> I want to do the job in swingers' clubs where you get to scatter condoms from the ceiling.

My account had barely any followers, and I didn't get any likes. I had to assume that people didn't know how to respond to a more or less bedbound woman with a serious disability who's constantly tweeting things like:

> In another life, I'd like to work as a high-class prostitute.

Or:

I'd have liked to try working at McDonald's.

I'd have liked to see what it was like to be a high school student.

I'm a 165 cm woman born to tall, attractive parents with platinum credit cards. If I wasn't disabled, the world would have been my oyster . . . whatever that means.

Funny to think that I was born and raised in Kanagawa and yet I've only been to Tokyo a handful of times (apart from Machida, which doesn't really count . . .).

I stopped being able to walk before they introduced automated ticket barriers, so I've only ever used the kind with a guy punching holes in your ticket.

When I went on overseas holidays as a kid we always flew business class, and yet I've never even ridden the bullet train.

While the care worker who came in at 1 P.M. was preparing my lunch, I got out of bed and disconnected from the ventilator, for good this time. Group Home Ingleside, the facility in a converted block of studio flats in which I was living, had been left to me by my parents as somewhere that I could live out the rest of my days. A single bedroom about sixteen square meters in size, along with a kitchen, toilet, and bathroom—this was the entirety of the space around which I could walk on my own two legs. I never once left the building and had no visitors, aside from the care workers, the care manager, the visiting staff members, and those working for the ventilator rental company. On clear days, the peak of Mount Fuji was faintly visible from my west-facing floor-to-ceiling window, but west lay to the right, meaning I couldn't turn my head in that direction. In the afternoons I'd sit in my set position behind the large desk, my back to the bay window with its ruffled balloon valance. There was a fifty-inch TV screen on the wall in front of me, but I rarely turned it on. Instead, I'd sometimes listen to the sounds of the TV in the room next to mine, which came leaking through the wall. At 2 P.M., my next-door neighbor would always watch an episode of one of the Korean drama series hovering around the top ten TV shows on Netflix.

Creating a hole right in the middle of your throat lessens the physical burden of breathing, it will be easier on the body than breathing through the nose and mouth, the lead doctor on my ward had explained to me when I was fourteen. Since I'd been given my tracheostomy, I had only needed to use the ventilator when lying on my back. Myotubular myopathy isn't degenerative—such had been my parents' beloved mantra, which they intoned in a manner that suggested it was something to be immensely grateful for. For me, though, this came as scant consolation. A genetic error meant that the blueprint for my muscle tissue was flawed. There might have been no dramatic degeneration, but that didn't alter the fact that my muscles were incapable of growing, maintaining themselves, or aging in the same way as those of someone without the condition.

To achieve a posture that put as little strain as possible on my twisted neck, I arranged my folded legs like puzzle pieces on the seat of the chair, then started up the laptop placed on the left-hand side of the desk. In the distance-learning degree program at the rather well-known private university in which I'd been enrolled for three years now, I earned an attendance credit by viewing an on-demand video, then participating in a discussion via an online forum with my thirty or so classmates. This was the second distance-learning degree I'd done.

I'd dropped out of education after middle school, and the first university I'd attended was one with a special system in place that allowed people to enroll without high school qualifications, so long as they took a certain number of credits in advance. I'd then hopped over from that less reputable distance-learning course to this one. I would often say to myself that I was engaged in a kind of qualification laundering. Yet for me, leaving aside my dabbles with armchair journalism, university was the only aspect of my life that offered any kind of connection with society. The other labels that granted one instant recognition— the kinds of occupations displayed in a list of options in a drop-down menu, like "office worker" or "housewife"—were inaccessible to me. This was why, even past the age of forty, I forked out large sums of money so that I could continue to cling to that seven-letter word: "student."

The posture that didn't put a strain on my neck put a strain on my lower back instead, so after thirty minutes I let my legs down into a position that eased my back. In another thirty minutes my neck would grow numb, so I'd fold my legs back up into their standard jigsaw arrangement. All the while, gravity was doing its best to compress my S-shaped backbone still further. Sandwiched as they were between my twisted spine and the hard plastic corrective brace in which my torso was encased so as to better resist gravity's exhortations, my heart and my lungs used the pulse oximeter readings to make their feelings of constriction known, constantly. Whenever I saw cultural figures or comments on Yahoo news articles lamenting that this or that about the state of the world was "stifling" or "made it hard to breathe," I would think to myself that these people really had no idea what it actually felt like, not to be able to breathe properly. They didn't even know what a pulse oximeter from thirty years back had looked like.

Once I'd digested my late brunch and my head had cleared, I opened up the Media & Communication Studies forum on Moodle, and set about formulating my thoughts on the topic at hand:

We might not always be conscious of it, but whenever we see printed text, we know that there's someone out there who's written it. Be it the product descriptions in mail-order catalogues, captions for photographs, or the copy in rental property or job vacancy catalogues, all that stuff is written by someone, which incurs a cost. I've grown much more aware of that since registering on a crowdsourcing site and beginning to take freelance writing jobs. The remuneration for writing online content whose purpose is largely search-engine optimization— exactly the kind of "armchair journalism" that has long been lambasted for a deterioration in the quality of search results—is between 0.2 and 2 yen per character. Requiring no physical reportage and instead cobbled together from information available online, armchair articles can be produced easily in large volumes in order to push up pageview counts. On the site I work for, the most successful combination among male users is firsthand accounts of various adult entertainment venues or lists of top twenty pickup spots, together with adverts for dating and hookup apps, while among women, it's lists of the top twenty shrines to pray at for rekindling romance, together with adverts for psychic hotlines. Honestly, it makes me wonder just how many women there are out there intent on getting their exes back. Like, girl, forget about him and move on with your life. . . !? But anyway, the writers get paid around 3,000 yen per article, so it serves as a good part-time job for those with caretaking responsibilities or people with serious disabilities like me, who struggle to leave the house. My motivation isn't a financial one, so I donate all the money I earn from penning these questionable articles to food banks, shelters for young girls with no homes to go to, or charities for orphaned children.

If we had some furikake to sprinkle on our rice then it'd feel like a meal—ever since I'd seen those words written on the food bank wishlist, I'd been sending them a boatload of furikake sprinkles that I ordered from Amazon. I knew how they felt—furikake was an indispensable item for getting through the tasteless meals that they served here at the group home, too. I guessed furikake was one of those things that saved people regardless of their financial status.

I owned the group home outright, and I was also paid income from rent by the management companies of several other apartment buildings that were in my name. The money that I'd inherited from my parents still lay untouched: several hundred-million lumps distributed across various banks. There was nobody to inherit from me, so after my death, the money would all go to the state. I often heard of cases where parents had worked hard to leave plenty behind to provide for their disabled children, but because those children had died without ever having kids of their own, it all went to the treasury. If those who were so aggrieved by disabled people not contributing to society and gobbling up everyone's benefit money knew about this, would it assuage their concerns a little?

I went to the bathroom, made an instant coffee, and returned to the desk. I waited for my oxygen saturation to reach ninety-seven, then picked up my iPhone.

I'd like to know what it's like to have an abortion.

I thought about it for a while, then saved that tweet in my drafts. I opened up Evernote on the browser of my laptop. I used this to spill out the more incendiary thoughts I had, giving them time to cool off.

I want to get pregnant, then have an abortion.
I can't imagine a fetus growing properly inside this crooked body of mine.
I guess I couldn't withstand labor either.
And of course, taking care of a baby would be out of the question for me.
But I could get pregnant and have an abortion like anybody else. There's no issue with my reproductive functions.
So I'd like to experience what that's like.
My ultimate dream is to get pregnant and have an abortion, just like a normal woman.

During the periods when Covid-19 was rampant I would of course stay inside my room, yet as the daughter of the people who had set up the home I felt a little guilty if I didn't use any of the facilities into whose creation so much money had been funneled, so as a rule I took my dinner in the second-floor dining room. My Yamaha electric wheelchair had an OB Mini suction unit attached, which was suitable for external use. Even when I was away from the ventilator, I couldn't be without a device to suction away mucus. As long as there was a plastic foreign object in the form of a tracheostomy tube stuck down my throat, my mucus membranes kept up a valiant attempt to fight it, and on account of their flawed blueprint, my respiratory muscles couldn't even produce a cough with any real propulsive force.

"One of the relatives of Mr. Tokunaga on the first floor brought us a great big bag of grapes," the care worker Suzaki informed me as she served me the tray with my dinner on it.

A small dish with three Kyoho and three Pione grapes had been appended to the tray as dessert. The main meal was mackerel cooked with miso, served with white rice, macaroni salad, and miso soup. I had forgotten to bring the furikake from my room.

With the eyes suspended above my mask set to Smile Mode, I nodded at Suzaki, hoping with that simple gesture to convey something along the lines of: "Grapes! Wow, I guess autumn's really on its way! Please pass on my thanks." I'd send a message in the residents' group chat afterward, conveying my grati-tude.

If the opening of my trach was covered then I could speak, but it put a strain on my throat and in-creased the amount of mucus I produced, so mostly I didn't. I only used verbal communication for things that couldn't be conveyed with a nod or a shake of the head. When my sentences grew too long I'd run out of breath, so I conducted any complicated conversa-tions by text.

Sitting diagonally three rows away from me, Ya-manouchi, a quadriplegic man in his fifties, was eat-ing his dinner with the aid of a care worker called Tanaka. Turning in their direction, I bobbed my head twice, slightly altering the angle of my head between bobs. Both nodded back. Yamanouchi, who had for-merly been a gifted car salesman, loved to talk. Now, he was holding forth endlessly to Suzaki, who had been working in the home for a long time.

"Still, I guess I'm lucky I was kicked out of work-ing society before the rise of digitalization and so on. I was hopeless with computers, even when my arms still worked!"

A spoon loaded with macaroni salad had been

hovering patiently in front of Mr. Yamanouchi's face for a while now, as he chattered away between his bouts of chewing.

"Right, and nowadays the controls are all on a touchscreen! I borrow my son's car and I've no idea how to use it! I can't even turn the radio on."

Suzaki, who always ended her sentences with a little chortling sound, was a master in the art of modulating the atmosphere to a major key.

"That said, I'd like to give that VR thing a try. You can go wherever you want in the world with just a pair of glasses, they say?"

"Oh yes, that sounds just great, doesn't it! Do you use VR and all that sort of stuff, Shaka?"

I shook my head. I'd never kept up any game for very long, whether on a console or online, and the prospect of opening up the cardboard box for a VR headset and then disposing of it was a pain.

"You've got all kinds of flashy new devices in your room, though, haven't you? What was that one you bought recently—a book scanner? How's the dissertation going, is it hard work?"

I nodded a nod designed to say, "Yeah, I'm finally getting close to picking a topic, but that's as far as I've got."

"You need one of those machines, too, Tanaka!" said Suzaki. "You're always reading manga on your iPhone."

"Oh, in the break room?" chipped in Yamanouchi. "Let me have a read next time, Tanaka! Is that *Kaiji* one still going?"

"I don't read it."

It was unclear from Tanaka's response whether he meant he wasn't reading Nobuyuki Fukumoto's *Gambling Apocalypse: Kaiji*, or that he didn't read manga in the break room at all. I imagined that a man in his thirties like Tanaka wouldn't be too concerned about owning manga for himself, and would likely be content with a manga-reading app—maybe one of the ones where you could read the manga for free if you waited for a while after it came out. Or the ones that allowed you to scroll through vertically.

Tanaka was wearing a mask, but the moment he said something at close range Yamanouchi instantly reproached him, saying, "Covid! Covid!"

Never mind that he himself was jabbering away like anything as he chewed his food.

Saying nothing, Tanaka dipped the rice he'd scooped up in the spoon into the miso sauce, as Yamanouchi liked, then brought the spoon, together with the bowl, up to his mouth.

Helping the garrulous Yamanouchi with his meals took patience. There was also the ever-present risk that his food might go down the wrong way and cause pneumonia. That said, this was a group home, which meant doing away with the type of oppressive control and inflexible rules characteristic of the institutions of bygone ages.

"Although what I really miss, even more than manga, is pachinko."

"Ah, I wish I could take you along one day, even if you couldn't play. Just to give you a taste of the atmosphere."

"The atmosphere!? That's not gonna do it! Still, these days I can't even flick my own balls, so I guess there's not much hope for me . . ."

Here it was—the self-deprecating humor of the afflicted.

"Stop it, Mr. Yamanouchi! You're in the company of a young lady, remember!"

"Ach, sorry."

I drank down a mouthful of miso soup with a serious expression, my head slightly cocked. I was born in 1979, which meant I was far beyond qualifying as "a young lady." Yet it was true that, having got my first period at nineteen, I still didn't look as if I were in my forties. Perhaps when my growth curve had veered off from that of a normal person, it had begun to trace an S-shape like my spine.

Having pacified the atmosphere for us, Suzaki retreated into the kitchen to serve up dinner for those service users who didn't come to eat in the canteen, then shuffled off down the corridor carrying a tray.

The atmosphere shifted to a minor key, and as I sat there in the now-hushed canteen I thought about whether the tweet that I'd put on ice before would stay at room temperature if I released it into the world, or if it would generate friction. For me, even this small canteen constituted a public space. It constituted society. Outbursts that ran counter to society's rules disrupted its rhythm. They startled people, in the same way that my ungainly limp did. Speaking about one's desire to kill a fetus was of a different order of magnitude to the lighthearted dirty jokes of a fifty-six-year-old man with a spinal cord injury.

Of course the tweetings of a hunchbacked monster would be more twisted than those of someone with a perfectly erect spine.

With my eyes on the effortlessly straight spine of the young man pressing a peeled Kyoho grape into the mouth of the man who could only move from the head upward, I snapped the backbone of the miso mackerel I'd just eaten cleanly in half with the tips of my chopsticks.

I MOVED THE SIX GRAPES I'd been given for dessert onto a tissue laid out on my desk. There wasn't much space to the left of my laptop, and one of the Kyohos plummeted tragically to the floor. I moved around to the chair behind the desk and sat down, then devised a plan.

I pulled another tissue from the box, which I scrunched up and opened out, then set down in the large space on the right-hand side of the desk. Retrieving the grabber that was hung on the bag hook to one side of the desk, I used it carefully to pincer the grape waiting impassively on the floor. Just about managing to maintain my grip on the grabber's handle with my right hand, I lifted up the grape, moved it over the undulating surface of the tissue, and let it drop. We were far past three-second territory—it was more like three minutes that the grape had been on the floor, and it would by now be riddled with germs. I folded it up in the tissue and threw it into the trash can.

Even when moving about inside this one-room apartment of mine, I always planned each and every movement meticulously before getting up. There was a constant danger of suffocating on the mucus I'd not managed to siphon away, and even leaving the issue of secretions aside, my oxygen saturation would plummet if I carried on moving for too long. Now I stood up to go to the bathroom, which, for efficiency's sake, I would have done on the way back from the canteen had I not been carrying the grapes, then made a mug of green tea from a tea bag and carried the steaming cup over to my desk, spilling much of its clear top layer as I went. *Careful not to fall, Shaka*— with the echo of my mother's voice enveloping me, I set about putting together the jigsaw puzzle of my bent legs on the chair top. The mug I used three times a day would be washed up by the care worker the following afternoon. The schedule that I'd been sent had Tanaka down for tomorrow. On Monday and Friday afternoons it was always Suzaki, while the other days left room for more flexibility. Mondays and Fridays were the days when I would be given a shower and hair-wash, so it had to be a care worker of the same gender. Having someone of the same gender to supervise my bathing was something that my parents had insisted on to the home's management. They understood the issues with staff shortages facing care facilities, but as parents, it was their dear wish that their daughter's dignity would in some way be preserved.

By this time of day, it was rare for my lungs to feel clear. Usually, the mucus that my crushed right lung was incapable of expelling by itself would have become trapped inside, causing the lung to partially collapse. The best thing for me to do would be to brush my teeth and then connect up to the ventilator already, but I hadn't yet met my daily target for the reading material that was too heavy to carry with me into bed. According to *The History of the Body*, edited by Corbin, Courtine, and Vigarello, the "criminalization of the gaze" that took hold around the dawn of the twentieth century had led to the decline of the freak show, which was subsequently replaced in popularity by the Monsters of Hollywood. Now, with costumes serving as an ethical cushion, people could enjoy ogling deformity without guilt or reserve.

Holding in both hands an open book three or four centimeters in thickness took a greater toll on my back than any other activity. Being able to see; being able to hold a book; being able to turn its pages; being able to maintain a reading posture; being able to go to a bookshop to buy a book—I loathed the exclusionary machismo of book culture that demanded that its participants meet these five criteria of able-bodiedness. I loathed, too, the ignorant arrogance of all those self-professed book-lovers so oblivious to their privilege. Pain shot through my heavy head, which my bent neck could only just about support. With the forward incline of this reading posture, my lower back, arced so as to crush my internal organs, lost its tug-of-war contest with the earth. Each time I read a physical book, I could feel my backbone bending a little bit farther. I had been in my third year of primary school when it had first begun to curve. I had always sat very upright at my desk in the classroom, my spine perfectly erect. Around a third of the children in the classroom with me would contort their spines into strange configurations so as to fix their eyes on their notebooks as they copied down what was on the blackboard. And yet, the one who ended up in the rehabilitation unit of the university hospital, surrounded by middle-aged men plying her naked body with plaster of Paris, was me. The spines of all those healthy kids with their bad postures didn't bend a smidgen. After all, their bodies housed the correct blueprints.

Where I'd grown up, almost none of the children's parents owned houses of their own, except for maybe the kids whose parents ran construction businesses. A military base town robbed of its name, whose blue sky was clouded over by the sound of warplanes. The kid with the gold miniskirt. The kid with the dolphin earrings. The kid who gave me a book written by the founder of the religious sect they belonged to. I don't expect that those children grew up to lead exceptional lives, but at least they're living in accordance with correct blueprints that don't cause their spines to bend. How could I, with only these mistaken blueprints to refer to, ever hope to turn out like them? I wouldn't object to living life on their level. Getting pregnant, having an abortion, breaking up, getting with someone new, getting pregnant, having a baby, breaking up, getting with someone else, having another baby—I'd be perfectly content if my life was just an imitation of that process.

I wanted to catch up with those kids, catch up with their backs. Even if I couldn't give birth, I wanted to get as far as aborting.

—

TANAKA APPROACHED MY DESK holding a melamine plate. I nodded at him in greeting.

"Your lunch," he announced through his mask after setting the plate down, then went over to the washing machine.

He crossed the room again with the laundry basket in hand, then stood by the balcony, hanging up the washing. Observing him out of the corner of my eye, I removed the butter dish from the mini fridge at my feet. I cut off a sliver from the hard yellow lump and placed it alongside my toast. Two sausages, a fried egg, and a gherkin—it was more like breakfast than lunch. My routine hadn't changed from when I lived at my parents' house. The only difference was that the care workers did the tasks previously performed by my mother.

As I was staring at the idle black of the TV screen, which reflected only the dust dancing through the air and my long, myopathic face, listening to the sounds of the Korean drama seeping through the wall, Tanaka moved to stand in front of the desk.

"You want something?"

I shook my head.

Yet Tanaka remained there, unmoving. I guessed

his work was done for the day—until he came to bring in my laundry in the evening, that is.

I cocked my head.

"The donation," he said, in a voice as devoid of feeling as the bright white of his disposable mask. His skin was of a similar pallor, which made his old acne scars stand out.

The donation. . . ? Oh, I thought, he must be referring to the discussion in the staff group chat that morning.

> I'm thinking of donating a VR headset
> to the communal space

my message had read.

> But I guess we'll need someone who
> knows how to use it, to help everyone out.

> I reckon Tanaka could figure
> it out?

the manager, Ms. Yamashita, had replied.

Her message had been read by everyone in the group, but Tanaka hadn't responded.

Was that what he was talking about?

"As a disadvantaged person you don't need to put yourself out like that, regardless of how much money you've got."

It was as he uttered this sentence, fairly long by his standards, that I noticed for the first time the way he was glaring down at me, his eyes narrowed into a look of contempt. Was this a new development? Or had he been looking at me like this all this time?

"I'm a beta male, okay. I'm one of the disadvantaged ones, too. So please don't make things more difficult for me than they already are."

Oh my god, I thought immediately, he's a creep. He's self-identifying as a beta male. He's probably an incel. Fuck!

The creases inside my mind channeled themselves into lines that together formed an emoticon smirk. I had no intention of letting it show on my face.

"Sorry," I said, covering my trach opening so I could speak. "I'll let it go."

Even graced by the rare sound of my voice, Tanaka didn't so much as nod. He shot a glance at the overhead scanner sitting on the desk, then left the room.

It struck me that if our interchange had taken

place between two non-disadvantaged parties, the script might have continued as follows:

—How do you use that?
—You open this bit up, place a book under-
neath, and set it to automatic mode, and
then it takes scans of the pages at five-
second intervals for you. It gets rid of your
fingers holding the page, as well.
—Wow, that's pretty handy. Sometimes it
feels like most of my living space is taken
up by my comics.

The conversation that sprang to mind had a sterile feel about it, like some kind of undercover marketing material. Still, finding meaning in the act of conversation, sterile or not, was the sign of those with well-developed communication skills. I knew that all too well.

What had taken place between Tanaka and me wasn't a conversation, but an attack. Why was it my lot in life to suffer attacks from a beta male? Though I could understand well enough what he was getting at.

I looked through the window to the washing rail on the balcony, where my sheets, towels, and clothes had been hung out neatly to dry. My underwear I washed by hand, tossed into the dryer, and put away at nighttime, so there was none of that out there. The tasks that the care workers assigned to my room had to carry out were relatively easy in comparison to those needed by other severely disabled people in the home. I didn't use a bedpan or diapers, and I didn't need lifting or feeding.

Maybe it was because of that that he'd misconstrued the distance between us.

Irritation and contempt were, after all, not things one felt for people far removed from oneself.

The hatred I felt for physical books obeyed the same logic. I felt no contempt toward the iron bars and jungle gyms in parks, for instance, however much they shunned my resolutely unathletic body.

Leaving half of my lunch on my plate, I started up my laptop. I watched the recording of a lecture on assistive technology, where the face-to-face students had no grasp of the differing requirements for input devices needed by those with cerebral palsy and those with muscular disorders. Someone with cerebral palsy who was affected by involuntary movements would want a stabilized input device, with a decently chunky joystick. Those with muscular disorders who were lying flat or at an incline would want a touch pad that they could place freely on their chests. The students in the video got this wrong, although it had been explained to them in the previous lecture, and the one before that, too. I assumed they had never laid eyes on a disabled person.

In American universities, in accordance with the stipulations of the Americans with Disabilities Act of 1990, not only are digital educational teaching resources the norm, but it's also compulsory for textbooks to be accessible to the visually impaired through a reader. Japan, on the other hand, works on the understanding that disabled people don't exist within society, so there are no such proactive considerations made. Able-bodied Japanese people have likely never even imagined a hunchbacked monster struggling to read a physical book. Here I was, feeling my spine being crushed a little more with every book that I read, while all those ebook-hating able-bodied people who went on and on about how they loved the smell of physical books, or the feel of the turning pages beneath their fingers, persisted in their state of happy

oblivion. A disabled TV personality had once dis-
cussed this issue of reading accessibility—I couldn't
now recall if it was on NHK Educational TV's *Barrier-
Free Variety Show* or Heart Net TV, NHK's social
welfare arm—but she had died just the other day
from a heart problem. On air, she had spoken elo-
quently about the difficulties she had with physical
books, which she couldn't read unless she had a carer
there to turn the pages for her. Yes, all those able-
bodied people didn't know how good they had it.
They could make erudite-sounding pronouncements
about how they just liked the smell of books, or the
feel of the paper, or the sense of tension that came
from the thickness of the remaining pages reducing
beneath their fingers, and others would listen unques-
tioningly to what they were saying. I wrote now on
the forum:

> The publishing industry is rife with ableist
> machismo. The world of sports, which all those
> literary types who play up their physical weak-
> ness display so much vitriol for, has in fact
> done far better at affording a space in its cor-
> ner for those with disabilities. What has the
> world of publishing ever done for the disabled

community? In 1975, a group of authors
launched a protest about a recorded-book service that one library had introduced for the visually impaired, resulting in its dissolution.
Those are the kinds of things that the literary
world makes a stand about. Just think of the
stagnation caused to the reading situation for
blind people because of that! In France,
meanwhile, it's been obligatory for publish-
ers to provide text data for all books for
years . . .

Mmmm! . . . Mhm . . . Aaah! Mhm!! MMmmMMM-
mmmHHH . . . AAAHHHH!!!!

From nine in the evening until three in the morning, with my lungs connected to the ventilator and an
iPad mini in my hands, I read and wrote. Having polished off the second half of the swingers' club article,
I used a text editor app to work on an erotic novel that
was being serialized on a writing site. The novel was
of a genre called Teens' Love, or TL for short: erotic
fiction written for women. If the content of the story
fit into popular categories such as "Eligible Bachelor," "Princess," "Medieval European Fantasy," etc.,

then it would fly up the rankings and publishing house editors would get in touch. Sex sells, as Toru Muranishi—aka the Emperor of Porn—attested. Was it Detective Sawazaki from Ryō Hara's crime novels who said that the only occupations you can take up overnight are those of politician and prostitute? Well, I'd add Teens' Love author to the list. The dribbles of royalty money from the ten or so ebooks that I'd released under the pen name Śākya rolled into my bank account each month, and immediately rolled out again to pay for a stranger's school fees or furikake. A promiscuous paycheck, for sure.

I'd like to state on record that it's totally impossible to represent women's sex sounds in print. I'd say it's several orders of difficulty above kids screaming. It seems as though everyone struggles with it, and of late I've encountered more people on the erotica site using something called heart gasps, where you append heart marks to the end of the *aahh*ing and *mmm*ing. Something like:

AaahMm ♡ MmmMM ♡!

I don't find it very dignified, though, so I don't bother.

I do like having them do all the noises, though, regardless. And it helps boost the word count:

Mmm, mmm! Mn, mnn! Aaah! Ah, aah, mmm! MNNmmmNNN!

What a funny old ecosystem, where these meaningless sounds transliterated by a middle-aged, severely disabled virgin generate income by setting people's honeypots aquiver.

When you've got no money problems and plenty
of health problems, you end up living
a very chaste sort of existence.

Evernote was full of drafts for tweets I'd never actually posted. I considered changing their tone to a more formal register and posting them on the Disability and Queer Studies module forum, but then decided against that, too. We were currently learning about the reproductive rights and health of disabled women. None of the issues touched upon in the lecture had ever affected me. The sexual abuse and nonconsensual care by people of the opposite gender that ran rife in residential facilities for disabled people and muscular dystrophy wards; visually impaired women being advised by their parents and doctors to give up the babies they'd conceived; women in wheelchairs unable to evade gropers on trains—none of these things were part of my lived experience. Just as the lives of women with disabilities seemed to run along parallel tracks to those of able-bodied women, so Shaka in her Nirvana seemed to be living along another track again. The tracks might look as though they would meet, but in reality, they never did. Bequeathed all this money by my parents, I had no need to allow my broken body to be ground down so as to enter society. Neither my heart, nor my skin, nor my mucus membranes had ever experienced friction with others.

Instead of tormenting myself about the chastity of my existence, I selected one of the futures I'd dreamed up and tweeted it:

> In another life, I'd like to work as a high-class prostitute.

I had experienced what it was like to be a woman whose money had distanced her from friction; I wanted to become a woman who earned money through that friction.

I went to the bathroom and changed my panty liner, where writing the sex scene had left its trace in strings of see-through liquid, then slept for five hours. When I woke up, I had a text from Ms. Yamashita, the group home manager.

> Shaka, sorry to bother you, but about your bath tomorrow . . .
> I've just found out that Asakawa's PCR came back positive, and Suzaki's having to isolate because she's a close contact. It looks like there's several classes off at the school.

Suzaki's grandchild and Asakawa's kids attended the same primary school.

> Gah, it's finally happened! What a pain.

> I'll try to come in myself if I can, but I can't really stand up today, so I'm not making any promises . . .

> Please don't push yourself! I know
> this isn't easy for you either, hav-
> ing to sort everything out when
> you're in such pain . . . It must be
> really tough.

Yamashita's preexisting back pain had taken a sudden turn for the worse, and she'd been off for a week. The pain was so extreme she'd been unable to get up, and even the pain-relieving suppositories were having virtually no effect. Yamashita, who'd been managing the home since it was set up, had been poached by my parents from the home medical care department of the university hospital I was a patient at. She was a trained nurse, and was a year older than me.

> What can we do, though? You don't
> want a male care worker bathing
> you, do you? I'll try to get someone
> else in to help if I can . . .

The Ingleside staff was made up of three men and three women, Yamashita included. There were also nurses from the visiting nurse agency who would

come to tend to those bedbound medical care patients
who required suctioning during the night.

> You know what, I don't actually
> mind if it's a man. I know it was a
> big concern for my parents, but
> I'm not all that fussed.

Really . . . ?! I'm not sure about that.
Though I have to say, with times
being what they are, it's certainly
appreciated . . .

> With times being what they
> are, there's no real sign that the
> staff shortage situation is going
> to improve, is there? And I'm
> not even just talking about
> Covid.

I'm so sorry about all this, Shaka.
I'll see if we can get someone in to help.
If that doesn't work then I guess Friday
will be Tanaka.

Okay, that's fine.

At least Tanaka is a diligent worker,
so in that respect you're in safe
hands.

Exactly.

We wrapped up the chat with a volley of stickers saying *Get Well Soon!* (her back pain) and *Hang in There!*
(my studies).

I didn't disagree with the assessment that Tanaka
was a diligent worker. But what did that signify in this
context, exactly? Was he going to wash every inch of
my body with the utmost diligence . . . ?

But he had to wash it, otherwise he wouldn't be
doing his job.

I was just getting him to do his job. That was it—
I didn't need to think on it any further.

With the same thumb that had closed the chat app,
I opened up the app whose logo was a white bird cut
out from a blue background, and pressed post on the
tweet that I had saved.

Next, I opened up the app synched with my other

devices whose symbol was a green elephant on a white background, copy-pasted all of the text about killing fetuses that I'd left there to marinate, and posted it as a thread of little sentences:

> My ultimate dream is to get pregnant and have an abortion, just like a normal woman.

There was no small irony in tweeting my dreams of being a normal woman with the very same fingers that had just authorized a male carer to bathe me, a command that would carry me ever further from the lives of normal women. I had to laugh. Nobody read my tweets anyway, so there was no risk of this going viral or anything.

In the afternoon, Nishi, my carer for the day, came to prepare my lunch, saying, "Honestly, it's still so scary, all this Covid stuff." Sixty-one-year-old Nishi had a kidney disease and needed dialysis three times a week, which doubtless only amplified his fear. I was scared, too.

"Oh, this came for you."

He placed an Amazon package down on my desk. I was already up and sitting at the chair by my desk, so I picked up the parcel between my thumb and forefinger and put it on the floor, leaning up against the wall. I knew what was inside: Shūji Terayama's *The Symbolism of Deformity*. I was only able to track down a secondhand copy through Amazon Marketplace. I had inherited my mother's fastidiousness about cleanliness and couldn't stand to touch secondhand books—which was why, after much deliberation, I'd bought a book scanner. I would always buy new books if they were available, even for specialist academic texts, which cost in excess of 5,000 yen. Library books were far too filthy for me to even countenance touching, and it wasn't as if I could physically make it to the library anyway. I didn't like having secondhand books in my house, but having professionals scanning them was illegal, so eventually I decided that yeah, okay, fine, I'd get a scanner and do it myself, happy now? I knew full well that the level of illegality was on a par with underage drinking or smoking, or selling fanfic manga at a comic convention, but here, again, my fastidiousness came into play.

With essay assignments I'd usually been able to get around it, but when it came to my dissertation, there was no avoiding secondhand books.

In the forum for the Culture and Representation Studies seminar group, the order in which we'd give presentations about our upcoming dissertations was soon to be announced. I was still struggling to decide on a topic. Should I write about anti-Semitism in the representation of the dwarf Alberich in Wagner's Ring Cycle? Or discuss the literature by Tomoko Yonezu and Gorō Iwama, the activists involved in the attempt to spray-paint the *Mona Lisa,* from the perspective of feminist disability theory?

Tomoko Yonezu had been a member of Japan's Women's Liberation movement. She walked with a limp in her right leg after contracting polio as a child. While I knew that I couldn't conflate our cases, I felt a great deal of empathy for her dousing the *Mona Lisa* with red spray paint while it was on loan at the Tokyo National Museum. At the time, the movement to reform the abortion law had given rise to a fierce conflict between women's groups who didn't want to give birth to disabled children, and disability advocates who didn't want disabled children to be killed. The two sides came together in a sort of Hegelian synthesis to take as their mutual enemy a society that left abortion as many people's only viable option. What emerged from this was the foundation of the reproductive rights of disabled women, and Yūho

Asaka's Cairo speech, where she proclaimed that the state was robbing disabled people of their right to have children. In 1996, the law was finally amended to acknowledge that disabled people could also reproduce, but the developments in reproductive technology and its commodification have seen the killing of disabled children become a relatively casual undertaking for most couples. In time, it will doubtless become even cheaper, even less of an event.

Given that, it wouldn't matter if a disabled person tried to get pregnant specifically to have an abortion, right?

Wouldn't that finally balance the scales?

I couldn't conflate my feelings with those of Tomoko Yonezu, who took out on the *Mona Lisa* the distress of a heart that was being ripped in two by the opposing forces of disability and able-bodiedness. I had my own reasons for wanting to vandalize that painting, though. I hated museums, and libraries, and any kind of historic building. I loathed old things, whose flawless, polished form had been impeccably preserved. I hated things that endured without breaking, that accrued value through aging. The longer I lived, the more my body collapsed into an ever more aberrant shape. It wasn't collapsing into death. Rather, it collapsed so as to live, collapsed as a testament to all the time I'd withstood. That made my disability decisively different from the fatal diseases or decrepitude of aging that the able-bodied might experience, where there was variation only in timing.

When I read a book my spine bends, crushing my lung, puncturing a hole in my throat; when I walk I bang my head—to live, my body breaks.

What is the difference between taking life from a body like that, over a body that flourishes to exist?

GRASPING THE WET HANDRAIL, I lowered myself down onto the shower chair.

The only thing I had on was a disposable mask. Even when it was Suzaki bathing me, it would always strike me how pervy it was to wear a mask while in the nude.

Tanaka, dressed in a blue polo shirt and shorts, picked up the showerhead and began to wash me, starting from my feet. The bowl in which my feet rested began gradually filling up with warm water. He'd let the shower run to heat up the water before I came into the bathroom—it was true, he was a diligent worker. From my legs he moved up to my stomach, torso, shoulders, then moved around behind me, washing my back. With no corset on, I propped myself up, clinging to the frame of the chair with arms straight as rods, keeping dead still. Setting the showerhead down, Tanaka lathered the soap with a washcloth, then supported my shoulders. The arms he scrubbed with the cloth were poles, just bone encased in skin. My chest, which the corset had prevented from developing, was like a vacant plot of land— a pair of brown nipples perched atop a set of protruding ribs. The reason that Mikio didn't like big-breasted women was that his mother had very large, pert breasts. My mother had been the same. My rib cage, which found itself thrust into the limelight after the leading actress had dropped out of the role, jutted out from my body with so much enthusiasm that it hung there like a sheer cliff face, with no landing in sight below. With my upper body floating in midair, the left side of my pelvis dug into my hollowed-out flank.

My upper back, my left leg, my right leg, the soles of my feet, the cracks between my toes—when he'd finished lathering every inch of my body in soap, Tanaka picked up the showerhead again and began to rinse it away. If water came in through the opening of my trach, I was in trouble. Tanaka stood his hand by my clavicle so as to shield it from the shower spray. I assumed that Suzaki, self-isolating at home, had sent him tips on how to do it.

I didn't look at Tanaka and had no interest in the expression on his face. I imagined he felt a similar disinterest toward my body. Unlike the nonconsensual care administered by the opposite sex that took place in heavy-handed healthcare facilities and hospitals, this was a situation I had consented to. Disabled people were not sexual beings—I had assented to the definition that society had created. To do so, I had fed myself a convenient lie. Fortunately, the times dictated I had to wear a mask, which prevented the lie from revealing itself.

I stood up so that he could finish rinsing me off. Now, at 165 cm in height, I found myself looking down at him.

Jun Tanaka: thirty-four years of age; 155 cm in height—I recalled reading these figures on his CV six months previously, and the lower lid of one of my eyes twitched. There was no need for me to remember such details, no need for me to remember his first name. His task impelled him to look up at me and our eyes met, but neither of us dropped our blank expressions. He passed me the showerhead, and while he was turned away, I washed my private parts in the usual order.

FRANZ LISZT WAS 185 CM in height, and it's said that his daughter Cosima was also tall. In fact, it has been suggested that there might have been as much as 15 cm disparity between her and her husband, Richard Wagner. Estimates of Wagner's precise height range considerably, from 150 to 167 cm, but there is no doubting that he was on the short side. The dwarf Alberich who places a curse on the Ring may have been the product of a hatred of his own kind.

Would I get away with writing a dissertation examining everyday lookism?

The input screen for the discussion forum was open in front of me, but my left hand stationed on the keyboard stayed still. I used my right arm to prop up my body, so touch-typing was out of the question.

In the right-hand corner of my vision, Tanaka was changing my sheets.

I suspected there were some fine dust particles or mites in the air, because I felt a tickling sensation in the mucus membranes of my windpipe and let out a few weak coughs, inaudible to anybody else. After coughing, I always had trouble breathing, and I'd have to suction several times an hour until I'd gotten rid of all the mucus. Occasionally, strands of my own hair would get into my windpipe through my trach. Transported by the cilia, the hair would slither its way toward my digestive tract and, until it finally crossed over my larynx, I would continue to choke so badly that I was rendered incapable of breathing.

"Can I ask you something?" Tanaka said, out of the blue.

I couldn't turn my head, so I flicked my eyes in his direction instead.

"How was the therapy?" he said without looking at me, still facing the bed.

The therapy . . . ?

The word "therapy," as it existed in the predictive text of my iPhone, denoted sexual therapy for women. I remembered tweeting something about it three months or so ago:

Now my parents are gone, I might as well start
investigating sexual services for women. Call it
therapy...

But no, there was no way that he could be referring to that, surely?

"The account called Śākya is you, right?"

The mucus transported up my airway by the pili
rose up into the trach tube, preventing me from
breathing.

"It's easy enough to track down, if you just search
for the names of the books you've read and the words
'group home.'"

I switched on the Minic suction unit, fitted the 6fr
suction catheter to the connector, and used a hand
mirror to insert it into the trach tube. I pumped it in
and out repeatedly to suction the mucus trapped in
my windpipe. In Japanese, the word meaning "pumped
in and out" would only conceivably be used by writers of erotica, but in China, from where it had been
imported into the Japanese language, it was a profan-
ity of ancient and honorable origin, even predating its
inclusion in the seventeenth-century erotic classic
The Plum in the Golden Vase.

These were the kinds of thoughts that pervaded

my brain, whether or not it was experiencing an oxy-gen shortage. Yet in my daily life, I passed for the young, silent, serious disabled woman Shaka Izawa. That was why I kept on releasing into the world all those vulgar, immature, unreasonable thoughts via my Buddha and Śākya accounts. Those words were born from the slimy, gunky sludge of the swamp, the mud out of which the lotus flowers grew. Without mud, the lotus could not survive.

My windpipe was now empty, at least until the next round of mucus rose up from my lungs. I covered my trach opening with my thumb, so that the air could pass to my vocal cords.

"I haven't gotten in touch yet."

Tanaka listened as he bent over to stretch out the folds in the sheet.

"Oh. So you just say whatever on there."

What was with that tone? Was he trying to sug-gest I was all talk?

More to the point, where had this sudden familiar-ity come from? Did he think that seeing me naked meant he was at liberty to alter the nature of our rela-tionship? For a brief moment, showerhead in hand, he had possessed absolute control over me. Was he feeling emboldened?

I breathed, conscious of a wheezing sound emanating from my lungs, then covered the opening in my trach again.

"You're interested in that kind of service?"

"Nope. I'm straight."

Tanaka went to bring in the pillow and summer duvet that were drying on the balcony. When he came back, I said in a slightly raised voice, "Then why do you ask?"

However you thought about it, there was only one way for this to shake out, and that was with blackmail. Except that even if Tanaka did use that shameless account of mine to blackmail me, I had virtually nothing to lose.

"Someone like that won't get you pregnant, though, will he?" Tanaka arranged the pillows, spread out the large towel over them, then replaced the pink Smile Cute Mini aspirator that he'd set to one side.

"Really?" I said somewhat desperately. Confronted with this point and caught off guard, I'd failed to properly think through my response. "They might say publicly that they don't, but I'm sure you can arrange it off record?"

I knew that such workarounds existed for men at sex clubs, after all.

"Are you that desperate to get pregnant? Or no, sorry. It's having an abortion that you're really keen on, isn't it?" For once, I detected feeling in Tanaka's voice. Namely, the contemptuous desire to view me as a perfect idiot.

"You must have things like that, though. Things that you really want, or want to do."

He scooped up the sheets, towels, and pajamas piled on the floor, carried them to the bathroom, and flung them into the washing machine. Suddenly, after all this time, it was hard to bear the idea that those items that soaked up my grime every night were being touched by a man's hands.

"I guess."

"Like what?"

Tanaka paused in front of my desk, and for the first time looked his interlocutor in the face as he answered.

"I want the kind of money you've got."

"What would you do with it, if you had it?"

"Dunno. I wouldn't give it away, that's for sure."

Tanaka shot a glance toward me as I sat there suffocating in the malicious words he had directed my way, then walked off to the end of the corridor. There he paused for just the moment it took to drizzle the words that were about to come out of his masked mouth with a phlegm green like olive oil. That was the color my mucus turned when stress caused the P. aeruginosa bacteria to win out.

"With that kind of money, you might be able to twist the sex therapist's arm, eh?"

I GUESSED THAT, ALTHOUGH it hadn't bothered me, it had him. He'd felt unable to say no. I wished that he had. If having to bathe me had caused him so much stress that it had rendered him incapable of concealing his animosity toward me, then I felt sorry for him. Yet it appeared as though his perusal of my Twitter account had been going on longer than just the last couple of days. Which made me wonder how much difference, in fact, my naked body had made.

He had agreed to bathe a woman with a severe disability for money, and while washing that deformed physique—a body he would rather not even have set eyes on—he must have felt as though he were polishing a heap of gold coins. Or maybe it went further than that—maybe he saw me, living as I was off the inheritance from my parents, as a pile of money that I hadn't rightfully earned.

Yet it was money that he couldn't access.

His words were like red spray paint.

Did that make me the *Mona Lisa* . . . ?

Gripping onto the edge of the desk with both hands, I coughed as my right lung was compressed by the wall of the corset. Viscous mucus had lodged in my deflated alveoli, preventing the air from getting in. Without it, I couldn't expel the mucus—it would remain there. Ambroxol and carbocisteine had only a token effect. *You need to drink more fluids, Shaka. The pulmonary surfactant that helps keep the alveoli inflated and softens the mucus has dried up.* No, Mom. You're wrong, that's not the problem anymore. The problem is that I've lived too long. My bones and my lungs have been comprehensively crushed. I've lived for too long with these flawed blueprints, and yet I was late to adulthood.

I picked out a 6fr catheter—the standard catheter size is 8fr, and the 6fr, which in pasta terms are roughly capellini-sized, are usually reserved for surgery—and pushed it all the way down my windpipe, driving it right down toward my lungs in an attempt to forcibly suck and drain the mucus that was refusing to come out. Yet even when I strained to cough, to dredge up the fluid from my lungs, nothing emerged. It occurred to me that maybe it would be the same for my baby—that it would resist with extraordinary stubbornness, that it would refuse to be scraped out of my womb. The thought was terrifying.

On a bathroom visit just before, I'd found strands of red in my underwear, which explained why I was dehydrated. I was just relieved that it hadn't come yesterday. In six days' time, I'd enter my most fertile period. Going by the folk wisdom that those whose periods started late were early to go through menopause, I probably didn't have that many chances left at becoming a person.

If he saw me purely in terms of my money, then I would regard him the same way.

Wasn't that how society worked, after all?

So, after waiting patiently for six days, I put the question to Tanaka.

"How much do you want?"

He grasped my meaning without any preamble. Such was the mutual understanding that existed between the disadvantaged. True, I'd never conceived of him in that way in the past, but his self-identification as such was all that I needed. People like us had no talent for conversation in a faintly sterile major key. Yet we were able to voice our truths in a minor cadence—or even a Schoenbergian discord. We stepped out of the preexisting frameworks and spoke our minds atonally.

As proof of this, Tanaka didn't allow any feigned confusion about the subject at hand to disrupt the tempo of the conversation.

"A hundred million," he said.

A cute figure, I thought. The back of my nose twinged with the urge to smile. I had an amount that I was struggling to work out what to do with after my death—it was slightly larger.

"How about 155 million?" I said, covering my throat. "Then it's proportionate with your height. One million yen for every centimeter. That's the price I'm willing to pay for your able body."

Then even if half of it was taken away by gift tax, it would still round up to 100 million—even if he understood that unspoken reasoning, the malice of what I'd said won out.

I could understand why he narrowed his eyes into a cast of contempt.

"You know that Yamanouchi's got plenty of semen, too? Does it have to be the sperm of an able-bodied person?"

He'd hit a sore spot. He may just have intended it as a dig, but unwittingly managed to strike right at the heart of my complex about being a woman with my disability.

"It's not that. It's that I . . . I can't go on top. You know what I mean."

I moved the lunch plate he'd just set down on my desk over to the top of my closed laptop, then took out a checkbook and a slightly yellowed checkwriter from my desk drawer. Even for a simple maneuver like that my movements were odd, my strengthless arms leaving me with no choice but to use my wrists and elbows like levers.

"Do you not want the 155 million?"

I pressed the bank seal I'd gotten out in preparation across the perforation line of the check and then tore it off. My hands trembled with guilt at the thought of putting my parents' money to such ridiculous use. My bank seal and bank book were usually secreted away in a location that only I knew about. In a group home where all the care workers had access to the master keys, and came and went between the residents' rooms, there was a limit to the level of security that could be attained, but if I made my inheritance my sole priority, what would I be left with? Whatever I did, nothing would remain after I was gone.

Tanaka didn't respond, so I plugged the check writer into the extension lead socket and set the check into the machine.

I tapped the keypad nine times.

"When?" Tanaka's gaze fell to my bed on his left.

"Now."

I slapped the signed and sealed check down on the desk, facing him.

He peered down at the asterisk at the end of the line of figures as if inspecting a speck of dirt.

"I'll come by when I've finished for the day. I'll make sure nobody sees."

THE MATTRESS THAT DIDN'T SO much as bounce when I sat down on it now sank with the weight of the man who'd seated himself on its left side.

"You hate it when men say 'Come over here, baby,' right?"

Hanging the mask he'd taken off on the bed's handrail, Tanaka smirked.

It makes my skin crawl when men say "Come over here, baby." Although of course I have to write it because it's all part of the established script . . .

Maybe things like this ended up happening to me because I took to my personal Twitter account to vent with such abandon my grievances about my job writing Teens' Love. In fact, my various attempts at armchair journalism—the blog where I chewed over trivial gossip about the group home residents; the diary I wrote about the sexploits of that Waseda student, S, that was featured as an ongoing series on an erotica site; in other words, all the trails of my dirty online secretions—would have been traceable from my Twitter account, if someone was so minded. This man knew the entirety of the fantasy world I had dreamed up under my assorted nomenclatures: Śākya, Shaka, Buddha. Now I understood what he'd meant when he said that it wasn't manga he'd been reading in the break room . . .

As I cowered in front of him, this avid follower of my Twitter account that nobody else looked at, Tanaka brought his mouth up to my ear and whispered into it, "Come over here, baby."

At least if it was his child, I'd be able to abort it without remorse. Of that I felt certain. I was sure, too, of the fact that the phrase pissed me off just the same whether it came from an eligible bachelor or a beta male like Tanaka.

"I wanna . . . drink . . . first."

"Do you drink? I've never seen any alcohol in here."

"No, that's not what I mean. I mean . . . your cum."

"Yeah, that's not a good idea." His delivery made it impossible to tell whether he meant the taste wasn't good, or it was a bad idea because he wouldn't be able to cum twice.

Kneeling on the bed, he unfastened the belt of his beige chinos. His unzipped trousers and boxers came off at the same time, and suddenly his genitals drooped there right in front of me, utterly uncensored, crowned by a bush of hair. Veiled in sweat after his day's work, they weren't all that different from those I'd seen in the gang rape scenes from the erotic manga that filled up my Kindle library.

I had the urge to cut a long strip of flavored nori to size and stick it on top, to serve as the censoring black bar that I was used to.

I took his cock between my thumb and index finger and put my mouth to its tip. It tasted salty. If a
mystery author were to commit the perfect crime in
real life, I thought, they'd doubtless find the experience hollow and saddening. I found I had sufficient
wherewithal to investigate the presence of scars with
my tongue. From the slight unevenness, I could tell
that he'd had the kind of circumcision that cost two to
three hundred thousand yen if you paid for it yourself, probably about five years ago. If you had it done
through health insurance it was much cheaper, but
the surgical procedure used in that case made the
whole thing much more obvious. So this was the kind
of thing he spent his money on, I thought. As I was
running my pointed tongue over the tracks of his
stitches, intending to trace them all, he grabbed hold
of my head and shoved himself fully inside my mouth.
Guessing that he would definitely be looking down at
me as if I were a piece of dirt now, I didn't have the
courage to look up. He used his hands to move my
head slowly and carefully from side to side, in a way
that I couldn't tell was for me or for him. It was easier
for me that way, in any case.

It worked just as it was supposed to inside my
mouth—I didn't know if that constituted a source of

humiliation for him. I felt sorry for him if it was. I could taste something that definitely wasn't my own saliva.

It was like I was sucking on his ressentiment, and it felt—good.

Because I didn't use my nose, mouth, or any part of my anatomy upward of my throat for breathing, there was no risk of suffocating, and I could perform the task at hand quite mechanically. The pumping in and out grew more intense, and as he moved my head around the way he liked it, he let out high-pitched strangled cries with little hearts at the end. Then the movement at the back of my throat stopped and he ejaculated.

That was bad news.

The warm, viscous liquid was almost impossible to swallow, and my feeble cough mechanism wasn't powerful enough to bring up the gunk that went sliding down my throat. As it neared the juncture with my esophagus, I began to choke, and my body folded over. That was where the choke reaction was at its most acute.

Leaving me spluttering and dribbling white-veined drool onto the towel that I'd pulled off the pillow, Tanaka turned away, and I heard his urgent, irregular footsteps growing more distant. Then the sound of the door closing.

Mucus surging up from my lungs came spilling out of my trach.

It was rare for me to choke this severely, but I was, nonetheless, used to it. Wholly unable to breathe, I clambered up beside the pillows on my bed and lay there while I used the suction unit. Then I connected to the ventilator. If it didn't turn on now, I'd die.

My lungs inflated, and the mucus bubbled up from inside. An hour later, when the bar spanning across the monitor indicating airway pressure had returned inside its normal range, I changed over the suction catheter. Before I threw the old one into the bin, I held the narrow pipe full of its glistening secretion up to the table lamp.

How much, exactly, had I paid per sperm, I wondered. It wasn't like they were killifish.

WHEN I WOKE THE following morning, I was feverish. My left lung had stiffened and was making a noise as though three baby mice were scurrying about in there.

This came as a shock—despite everything, I'd always had a good immune system, and barely ever came down with a fever, even as a child.

I tested negative for Covid, but the doctor advised that I should admit myself into the university hospital. In shifting to home medical care, I thought that I'd cut all ties with the place, but I was returning now to my former haunt once again. That said, I'd registered to donate my body to the university's medical society, so whatever happened I was set to return to the campus after my death. The airway pressure alarm on the ventilator chirruped endlessly.

I was diagnosed with aspiration pneumonia.

It took about a day for one of the three baby mice to emerge, and during that time, they seemed to have produced four more—just as one section of my lung had been freed up, another, larger chamber had been blocked off. There was nothing to do except slowly and steadily suction off the mucus raging tempestuously through my chest. I was thankful that, on account of the drip and the urethral catheter I'd been given, fluid kept flowing automatically through my body.

Tanaka's ressentiment was inflaming my lungs.

The manager, who stopped by to deliver a change of clothes the following day, was walking with a stick, still in evident pain. I felt an affinity with the way she was walking, one foot dragging slightly behind her.

"Are you okay, Shaka? Thank goodness it's not Covid! Oooh, these private rooms are pretty big, aren't they?"

"I'm sorry for worrying you," replied the mechanical voice of the app that read aloud the text you typed into its input box.

I'd already realized that, with just my iPhone on me, I'd be incapable of getting on with either my work or my university assignments. My breathing and my excretions were being taken care of by external devices. Once my fever had been brought down by the drugs, there wasn't that much difference between this and my regular, healthy state.

"I got held up at the home medical care department on the way here. Ando was singing the praises of the pain clinic."

This hospital was Yamashita's former home, too.

"You should go along. Take some time off and give it a try," said my app.

"Aw, thanks. I must say, I'm relieved that Ingleside seemed to function okay without me there."

"Postpartum back pain can go on for a while, can't it?"

"Honestly, it's such a drag. It's tough enough bringing up a six-year-old and a three-year-old without that in the mix."

Occasionally laying down the stick that she'd propped up beside her so as to access certain shelves, Yamashita efficiently loaded the things she'd brought for me into the closet, then, with her wallet in hand, said, "I'll go and get you something to drink and some jelly, shall I?"

The Covid-induced ban on visits had only just been lifted, and the allotted time was merely ten minutes.

"Can you get me some furikake, too?"

"Sure. Oh, and once you're better, I'll book you in for some swallowing therapy."

"I've never done that before."

"I think it's best that we have you do some proper training at least once. This has never happened to you before, after all."

The manager my parents had entrusted me with was indeed extremely dependable.

This helpless, hunchback monster, all alone in the world, understood very well what a blessing that was. Right, Dad? Right, Mom?

The reason that I gave away all the money I earned

was to redistribute some of the enormous privilege bestowed upon me to those whose lifestyles were less fortunate. Yamashita, who'd headed off to the convenience store with the trustworthy clunk of her cane, returned with an arrangement of yellow dried flowers. She brightened up the windowsill with them, filled the fridge with bottled green tea, and then went off back to Ingleside.

The hospital, where there was no concept of privacy and people came and went freely day and night, was not a good environment for engaging in either my dead-earnest studies or all the raunchy reading and writing I had to do for work, so I decided instead to reread L. M. Montgomery's *Anne of Ingleside* on my iPhone. This was the kind of person that the ever-so-chaste Shaka Izawa had started out her life as.

Ingleside was the name of the house where Anne lived together with her beloved husband, children, and housekeeper. In my girlhood, when I'd read the Anne of Green Gables series over and over, I'd never suspected for a moment that I would grow up in the future to become an old maid. And yet, my decision to call the group home "Ingleside" hadn't been an ironic one.

Two days on, when my lung was sheltering just a

single baby mouse, Tanaka was asked by the manager to bring my electric wheelchair to the hospital. This had to mean that nobody knew about what had happened, and he wasn't under suspicion.

Having placed the folded chair and basket by the entrance, Tanaka stood there motionless for about two seconds, a paper bag in his hand. I didn't know if it was the room he was looking at or me. The bag contained shoes.

He took them out without so much as a rustle, arranged them by the bed, and then stood up.

I narrowed my eyes, pretending to be concentrating on the description of Ingleside's ceramic mantel dogs, Gog and Magog.

"Do you need anything?"

I shook my head where it rested on the pillow.

My washing was being handled by the hospital's laundry service, so there was nothing for him to take back.

I can't yet remove my ventilator or go to the bathroom, so I imagine it'll be a while before I can leave— I had no inclination to while away time with regular, harmless conversation of that kind. I had no memory of engaging in that sort of talk with him before, when it had been Tanaka's day to care for me. He'd ask me if I needed anything and I'd shake my head silently—that was the tonal form that our conversation assumed.

"Was it worth risking your life for?"

He stood totally unmoving. The mask obscuring his mouth made him seem like a doll that had suddenly taken on the power of speech.

I gripped my iPhone like a weapon.

"The only thing you need to think about is the money."

The line of dialogue I wrote was so bad that even the mechanical voice seemed repelled, and read it aloud in a particularly expressionless tone. Feeble and corny. *You just focus on the money, okay?* would have been better. Or else, *Let's pick back up when I'm home.* I wish I could have spoken it like Misato from *Evangelion*. I still hadn't given up on the idea that Tanaka would do his bit to help me kill my fetus in exchange for money.

I hadn't known whether he really would come, so I'd shut the check away in my desk drawer. If he wanted to take it and run off somewhere while I wasn't there, then he could go ahead.

The thing I didn't want was for him to pretend as if nothing had happened.

I wanted him to be more vicious.

"I don't care if you hate me."

This line was less Teens' Love and more Boys' Love—narratives depicting relationships between men, marketed to women. There was no chance that I'd be able to win over a real-life man with such fictive dialogue.

Feeling the constraints of not having a real-life body of the kind that society approved of, I tossed my iPhone onto the waterproof sheet.

"Take care," he said, glancing down at my iPhone, then turned away and left the room. Just as when he was looking after me in the home, there was no goodbye, nothing.

Take care of what? My iPhone? My ailing body? Or else . . .

Even someone like me was capable of catching his drift.

TANAKA LEFT INGLESIDE BEFORE I was released from the hospital. I felt like I'd done the manager a disservice. In this time of such endless staff shortages, I'd managed to add to her concerns.

"My guess is that Mr. Yamanouchi objected to being cared for by a boy like that, and was taking it out on him."

Tanaka might have looked young but he was hardly a "boy," I thought to myself. Still, I supposed those kinds of judgments were relative.

The manager seemed to feel obliged to share this type of information with me, a habit that had been instilled in her before coming to the home. Now, in my bedroom with the things I'd brought back from the hospital almost tidied away, she pulled out the bedside chair that usually served a purely decorative purpose and sipped at a can of coffee that I'd picked up for her from the hospital convenience store on my way back from my rehabilitation session. The stuffed Snoopy that had been perched on the chair sat on her lap. I'd bought it forever ago from the duty-free shop in Guam, where my family had had a holiday home. I'd had it cleaned several times, but it turned gray with dust again almost immediately.

"He takes it for granted that he'll be cared for by a woman, you know? But from our perspective, male carers are good news, particularly for those with serious disabilities."

From the way that the manager craned her neck to look outside the window when she raised the can to her mouth, I could tell that there was a good view of Mount Fuji today. I couldn't see it while lying in bed.

"But the stress builds up in Mr. Yamanouchi's body, too. I feel like we need to give him an outlet of some kind."

I nodded, a serious expression on my face, but didn't offer any suggestions.

I bore no responsibility in any of this. With my reduced muscular strength, I couldn't afford to bear any.

Suzaki entered the room, asking, "Shaka, do you want to sit up to have your lunch?"

Yes, sure.

With myotubular myopathy, the muscles were quick to waste away if they weren't being used, and couldn't subsequently be recovered, no matter how hard you trained them. I could no longer climb the stairs although I'd once been able to. A year after having handrails installed by the toilet, I could no longer stand up without them.

And so, Shaka in Nirvana fought for dear life to get up from her bed, and sat at her desk until evening, day in, day out, however much suffering it caused her.

As much as she hated physical books, still she clung onto them with all the strength that she had.

From the other side of the wall, I heard a dry clap. The person in the next room, who had a similar sort of muscular disorder as me, was bedridden. When she'd finished using the bedpan, she would clap her hands, and the care worker waiting by the kitchen would come to clear it away. The people of the world averted their eyes as they said, "I couldn't bear it if that were me. I'd rather die than live like that." But that was mistaken. The way that the person next door lived was where true human dignity resided. That was the real Nirvana. I hadn't yet arrived.

Straining my ears, I made out the gradual swelling of a soft voice singing in Korean, a melody building toward romantic fulfillment. While in the hospital, I'd developed the habit of turning on the TV out of boredom. Now, I opened my drawer to search for the remote control.

But the TV wouldn't turn on.

I changed the battery and tried again, with no luck. When I looked carefully, I noticed that the power light on the TV was flashing in a way I hadn't seen it do before. I googled to see what the red flashing light signified. It meant it was broken.

The TV had broken while I wasn't using it.

I didn't have the strength to try unplugging it and plugging it back in again, so I returned the remote to the drawer. The check for 155,000,000 yen was still in there.

Right, yes. The appropriate distance between us was one that allowed him to pity me.

I couldn't become the *Mona Lisa*. I was, after all, a hunchback monster.

. . . it shall be in the latter days, and I will bring thee against my land, that the heathen may know me, when I shall be sanctified in thee, O Gog, before their eyes . . .

. . . and it shall come to pass at the same time when Gog shall come against the land of Israel, sayeth the Lord God, that my fury shall come up in my face. For in my jealousy and in the fire of my wrath have I spoken . . .

. . . and I will rain upon him, and upon his bands, and upon the many people that are with him, an overflowing rain, and great hailstones, fire, and brimstone . . .

... and I will send a fire on Magog, and among
   them that dwell carelessly in the isles: and
   they shall know that I am the Lord. So will
   I make my holy name known in the midst of
   my people Israel; and I will not let them
   pollute my holy name any more: and the
   heathen shall know that I am the Lord, the
   Holy One in Israel.

Behold, it is come, and it is done, sayeth the
   Lord God; this is the day whereof I have
   spoken.

....

THE FRIDGE IN the common room was always
crammed full of 7-Eleven food: zaru soba, onigiri,
and sandwiches. Since the time I'd gotten a bad stomach after eating a chilled onigiri, though, I'd started
buying my own from FamilyMart and bringing them
in. I liked the ones they sold at the co-op on the main
university campus best, but these days I only went
there once a week. I was sitting with my MacBook
perched atop my crossed legs, writing my trivial non-
sense and rubbing the rough umeboshi pit against the

side of my tongue that liked to be grazed like that, when a call came in. I quickly stuffed my closed MacBook into my bag. Rin, who had returned from one of the private rooms wearing a cardigan, shot me a pleading look and said, "Shaka, have you got any douches?"

"Sorry, I'm out too. Ask Sen to go get some!"

With that, I passed through the red dividing curtain into the hall. When I'd first visited this place to scope it out, I'd taken a liking to this crimson curtain, which looked as if a dwarf in a red suit might emerge from behind it at any moment, and I'd decided on that basis to give the job a shot. I just wanted to earn money in the easiest way possible, and I had no intention of being picky about the place, or the customers. I did find it freaky how the condoms always broke, though, even if Rin didn't seem to think so.

"Hello, I'm Shaka! ♡" I got a lot of repeat customers, but this guy was a first-timer. He was what we called a copycat—he'd come in after reading a review on the net. His face was yellowing, his hair thin, and he wore glasses, so that he looked quite a lot like a lanky Minion. His voice was a bit squeaky, too. He wasn't as cute as a Minion, though, so I decided to call him Minio. I felt like the sort of sex that suited me best was the kind where you got straight down to it, didn't use a condom, and finished up with a creampie. The clients knew that this was what the star mark alongside my headshot in the lineup meant, so the ones who requested me didn't tend to look for any nods toward an adventurous performance. Ultimately, you could make the most money from the guys who wanted to bareback an E-cup student with a nice face and shoot their load inside her.

"You're a literature student, you say? Yeah, I can see that."

Minio wanted to start by giving me a shoulder rub. I knelt up at the edge of the bed and let him massage me. This was pretty rare, but not unheard of. Apparently some people had a thing for it.

"Dissertation, eh? What kind of things do you write about for a literature thesis?"

In fact I was studying politics and economics, but that put guys off something rotten, so I was in the habit of sweetening it a bit and saying literature. Now I said the first thing that came into my head.

"I'm writing about representation of disability in the works of David Lynch."

"Wow. Don't really get it but it sounds hard."

Needless to say, Minio's yellow hands didn't confine themselves to my shoulders, but flapped around my upper arms as if trying to restrain me, then descended to knead my breasts from above my camisole. Did Minions have arms, I wondered to myself, and if so, what were they like again? Were they long or short?

"I don't really get it either, honestly. It's looking like I might not make the deadline anyway."

Minio had introduced himself as a systems engineer at a start-up, and I imagined that the only actions his fingers knew were flying across the keyboard and twiddling nipples. As he twiddled away at mine, he started breathing into my ears. A couple of hours ago a client whose breath smelled like the floating market on the Chao Phraya River had given my earholes a very thorough licking, so you're probably best off not getting too tonguesy, dude. . . ?

"What are you doing working a slutty job like this, when you're so smart and so beautiful?"

Huh!? Slut, did I hear you say. . . ? That's "goddess" to you, mister . . .

But I had this thing where I got a kick from having gross things said or done to me by gross people, so when Minio whispered this to me in his screechy voice, I felt my body quaking as I replied, "It's to pay for my tuition fees."

Having licked his way down from under my ears to the nape of my neck, Minio now asked in a weird crooning tone that was supposed to sound sympathetic, "You've got to pay your own way, you poor thing. What do your parents do?"

"Um . . ."

"Oh dear, I'm sorry. Did I make you remember something nasty, sweetheart?"

Minio, who seemed to have no qualms about fully inhabiting the middle-aged-man cliché, tugged my camisole up and took it off. Hey, it's a bit chilly today, my boobs complained.

"My elder brother's in prison."

"Huh?"

"Yeah, it happened when I was in middle school. It made my mom go funny in the head, and she joined some strange religion."

"Oh dear!"

"Gave away all our money to them. But she always had a real complex about her own grades at school, so the one thing she didn't donate was my education insurance."

Which was why I always studied hard, and got into the university I wanted first try, without any kind of commendation from my school. The reason I'd run out of money in my fourth year was mostly down to Tan, who worked at a host club. Today, once again, he hadn't texted. Such a bastard. Instead, I'd had a message from a trader I met at a swingers' club last week, inviting me to go and visit his company. I guess we'll end up at a hotel after, and I'm cool with that.

This newfound nymphomania of mine is also Tan's doing.

It's so effing unfair.

"That's not enough, though, is it? Shaka-chan, I'd like you to lick me all over."

This was an option on the menu that they had to pay extra for. Minio felt that by doing what he wanted with my body and coughing up three or four ten-thousand-yen notes emblazoned with the face of the founder of Keio University, he was contributing to my education. This ocher-skinned loser.

"What did your brother do?" he asked as I was straddling him and licking his armpits. There were clients who would plunge straight in and ask, and those who didn't. Then there were the ones who would ask as they plunged straight in.

"He killed a woman."

"Oh . . ."

"He joined a company straight out of college, but he got bullied and quit after six months. For a year or so after that he hung around doing nothing. But then he got his qualification as a carer, and worked for a couple of years at a nursing home, before shifting to working at a group home run by the same company. He killed one of the residents there."

Minio's response to this was so unclear— something along the lines of *guaargh* or *yurrrgh*— that I was taken by the urge to run it through an equalizer, but then this was pretty much par for the course among my clients.

"He wrung her neck until she told him where her bank book and seal were, then ran off with them. It was obvious that they'd find him right away."

"That must have been so hard for you."

Not half as hard as licking every inch of someone's body, I was on the verge of replying. That really takes it out of you.

When I got to the part of his thighs close to his balls, he started letting out horny grunts, lifting up his head to look at me, so I shot him a grin.

"But when I'm with someone like you, I can forget all about the horrible things that have happened to me."

I had him. The corners of his eyes and mouth melted like the edges of the cheddar square poking out the sides of a double cheeseburger.

"You're so great, Shaka!" he said as he stuck his middle finger inside me. Then he flipped me over and started sucking my tits.

What about the blow job that was part of the all-body-licking price packet? Or was he one of those guys who wanted it sucked after he'd cum?

"You're so wet already."

"It's because you're so kind."

After fumbling around down there with a similar brand of clumsy roughness to the others, he stuck it in without a word. I was beside myself that I hadn't heard from Tan for three whole days, but the cries I let out were those of a girl experiencing pleasure the likes of which she'd never known before. If this was opera, then I was performing a coloratura. The days when I'd done it with Tan the previous night I'd feel happy, but then the chasm between him and these awful clients depressed me so much that I could only let out the tiniest little invalid moans. It was all Tan's fault. I hated him. It was thanks to Tan that I had this sick feeling in my chest and felt so unhappy all the time. When I was at my unhappiest, I'd spend my time replaying the scenes of the sex we'd had on loop. I'd become able to orgasm without even touching myself.

I liked Tan's face, a whole lot.

But the trader's technique and rhythm were something I'd never experienced before.

Was I best off changing lanes? Would that make me happier?

Unlike Tan, would the trader treat me nicely regardless of whether I bought a bottle of his club's most expensive champagne?

"I've got a lot of time for a girl who likes a good creampie. But just be careful you don't end up as a single mother with a bunch of kids, repeating the poverty cycle, okay?"

"Yeah, no risk of that."

This wasn't actually true. The pill didn't agree with me, and I'd stopped taking it.

"Work hard on your dissertation, okay?"

"Okay."

"I'm gonna cum, okay?"

"Okay."

From the bright white of the ceiling, the dazzling round eye of the downlight stared down at me. I looked up at its brilliant light. On the other side of that light, lotus flowers bloomed. The flowers of Nirvana that blossomed out of the mud.

I could still remember the slightly unusual name of the woman my brother had killed, and the slightly unusual name of her illness.

At the time, in my second year of middle school, thoughts of her had haunted me every night. Even now, I still thought about her all the time. About the sort of things she'd felt up until that final day, about the things she'd seen on her last night.

The story I was writing was a means of surviving, of holding on to my sanity, within this family of mine that was crumbling apart.

Just as the stories that she wrote were a way for her to survive in society.

Maybe I have no brother—maybe I myself don't exist.

Down here in the mud, the seeds of life come falling from above, dazzling in their whiteness.

I GUESS THAT, SOMEDAY, I'll conceive the child that Shaka wanted to kill so that she might become a person. Maybe that someday is—now.

ACKNOWLEDGMENTS

Polly Barton would like to thank Kimihiro Tomioka, Yuji Nishino, and Motoyuki Shibata for their help and support, with this book and always. Huge thanks, also, to Saho Baldwin, Edward Kirke, David Ebershoff, Karen Whitlock—and, of course, to Saou Ichikawa.

SAOU ICHIKAWA graduated from the School of Human Sciences, Waseda University. Her bestselling debut novel, *Hunchback*, won the Bungakukai Prize for New Writers, and she is the first author with a physical disability to receive the Akutagawa Prize, one of Japan's top literary awards. She has congenital myopathy and uses a ventilator and an electric wheelchair. Ichikawa lives outside Tokyo.

POLLY BARTON is an award-winning translator and writer. She lives in Bristol, England.

This book was set in Fournier, a typeface named for Pierre-Simon Fournier (1712–68), the youngest son of a French printing family. He started out engraving woodblocks and large capitals, then moved on to fonts of type. In 1736 he began his own foundry and made several important contributions in the field of type design; he is said to have cut 147 alphabets of his own creation. Fournier is probably best remembered as the designer of St. Augustine Ordinaire, a face that served as the model for the Monotype Corporation's Fournier, which was released in 1925.